Fledge Star

Twink

Bimi

Pix

Sooze

Sili

Zena

Mariella

Lola

Book Five

Fledge Star

Titania Woods
Illustrated by Smiljana Coh

BLOOMSBURY

LONDON BERLIN NEW YORK

To Liz

Bloomsbury Publishing, London, Berlin and New York

First published in Great Britain in 2008 by Bloomsbury Publishing Plc
36 Soho Square, London, W1D 3QY

This edition published in 2009

Text copyright © Lee Weatherly 2008
Illustrations copyright © Smiljana Coh 2008
The moral rights of the author and illustrator have been asserted

A CIP catalogue record of this book is available from the British Library

ISBN 978 1 4088 0490 2

FSC
Mixed Sources
Product group from well-managed
forests and other controlled sources

Cert no. SGS - COC - 2061
www.fsc.org
© 1996 Forest Stewardship Council

Typeset by Dorchester Typesetting Group Ltd
Printed in Great Britain by Clays Ltd, St Ives Plc

1 3 5 7 9 10 8 6 4 2

www.glitterwingsacademy.co.uk

Chapter One

A new year at Glitterwings! Twink Flutterby flew eagerly over the flower-covered hill. Almost there . . . almost . . . and then, there it was! The great oak tree that housed Glitterwings Academy came into view, its leaves bursting with springtime. The tiny windows that wound their way up its trunk shone like pieces of sunshine.

'Isn't it beautiful!' exclaimed Twink's grandmother, flying beside her. She was accompanying Twink to school this term, as Twink's parents were at a Fairy Medics' convention. 'I can see why you love it so much, my dear.'

Twink nodded happily. 'It's the most wonderful school in the world.'

Down below, a first-year student rode on a mouse, with her parents flying along overhead. The young fairy glanced up at Twink admiringly, and Twink felt very grown-up all of a sudden. She and her friends were Second Years now – not the babies of the school any longer.

Twink and her grandmother landed on the Glitterwings front lawn. Gran carefully patted her purple hair into place. 'Now then,' she said, 'we just need to let someone know you're here.'

Crowds of young fairies flitted about the tree like hummingbirds, chatting and laughing. 'Twink!' called a voice.

Twink looked up as a strikingly pretty fairy with dark blue hair and silver and gold wings landed beside her. 'Bimi!' she cried, delighted to see her best friend.

The two girls hugged excitedly, their wings fluttering so hard that they lifted off the ground.

'It's so good to see you!' said Bimi as they floated back down to earth. 'Sending letters by butterfly just isn't the same. And guess what — we're going to be in the same branch together!'

Twink felt a wide smile spread across her face. 'Glimmery! Oh, we're going to have such a brilliant term, I can tell already!'

'Yes, excellent news,' said Twink's grandmother with a twinkle in her eye. 'But have you a hello for me as well, Bimi?'

Bimi's cheeks turned pink. 'Oh – sorry, Mrs Flutterby!' The term before last she had stayed with Twink's family for part of the holidays, and knew Twink's gran well.

'Quite all right,' laughed Gran. 'Now, let's get you sorted, Twink, and then I can fly my tired old wings back home.'

Their new year head was Miss Sparkle. The stern Fairy Dust teacher gave Twink a brief smile as she ticked Twink's name off her clover-leaf pad.

'Nice to see you, Twink. All you girls from last year are together again in Peony Branch, up near the

top of the tree.' Miss Sparkle turned away to check someone else in, her thin white wings almost transparent in the sunshine.

Twink's gran gave her a warm hug, and patted Bimi's cheek. 'Have a good term, girls. Don't get into any more trouble than absolutely necessary!'

'We won't,' grinned Twink as her grandmother lifted gracefully off the ground. She and Bimi stood waving until Gran had disappeared over the hill, and then Twink scooped up her oak-leaf bag. 'Come on! Let's go and see our new branch!'

The two friends took off at top speed. Giggling, they dodged past a group of older girls and jetted through the open double doors at the base of the tree.

Twink stopped and hovered for a moment, drinking in the beauty of her school. The inside of Glitterwings Academy was a high, golden tower, with branch-corridors shooting off in all directions, and fairies flitting about as far up as the eye could see. Twink sighed happily. She could never get tired of seeing this, no matter how long she had gone to school here!

'Hurry,' called Bimi over her shoulder, 'or else we won't get beds next to each other!'

Jolted out of her reverie, Twink sped to catch up with her friend. Up and up they flew, passing classrooms and sleeping branches as they went. Twink felt a slight pang as they flew past Daffodil Branch, where they had lived last year.

'Good old Daffy Branch!' said Bimi affectionately. 'I'll miss it, won't you?'

Twink nodded. 'It doesn't seem right to think of anyone else living there. But I bet we'll like Peony Branch, too.'

The trunk narrowed as they neared the top of the tree. 'Look, there it is!' cried Bimi. A large peony hung upside down over the branch entrance, its petals a rich, vibrant pink.

'How pretty!' breathed Twink as they landed on the ledge. She eagerly pushed open the door, and her eyes widened. Their new branch was beautiful!

It curved gently to one side like a beetle's wing, with a whole row of windows sparkling in the sun.

Green, mossy beds awaited each fairy, with a peony hanging over each one like a frilly canopy. Several of the other girls had arrived already, and were busy unpacking their things.

'Opposite!' shrieked a voice. A lavender-haired fairy launched herself at Twink like a whirlwind, hugging her hard. 'What do you think?' she demanded, jumping up and down. 'We're all together again!'

'Hi, Sooze,' laughed Twink.

Sooze had lavender hair and pink wings – the exact 'opposite' of Twink, who had pink hair and lavender wings. The two fairies had been best friends once, and Twink still liked Sooze, though she knew she had the best friend in the world in Bimi now. Unlike Sooze, Bimi could be counted on, no matter what!

Across the branch, a pointy-faced fairy with light green wings sniffed. 'Well, *I* rather fancied a change. I told my mother that I wanted to be in Orchid Branch this term, but the school still put me in here.'

Sooze smiled impishly. 'Why, Mariella, what a coincidence! We fancied a change from *you,* as well. Are you sure you begged and pleaded hard enough?'

Mariella glared at her and whispered something to Lola, the thin little fairy who was her only friend. Lifting their noses, the two fairies turned away, fluttering their wings grandly.

'Some things never change, do they?' grinned Twink. 'Come on, Bimi – let's take those two beds over at the end.'

She happily unpacked her oak-leaf bag, arranging the drawings of her family on her bedside mushroom. Her parents and little sister smiled out at her. Teena was very proud to have a big sister at Glitterwings Academy – and wild with impatience to start there herself next year.

Twink placed her thistle comb and a bottle of wing polish on her bedside mushroom as well, and then arranged her petal notepads in the bark cupboard beside her bed. 'There!' she said with satisfaction. 'Are you finished, Bimi? Let's go and have a look around before the welcome back session in the Great Branch.'

Bimi laughed. 'Nothing will have changed in only three weeks, you know!' But she shut her bark cupboard and the two fairies flitted lightly from the branch, circling downwards.

A crowd of first-year students were just making their way up the trunk, riding on the backs of grey and yellow tits. Twink had to smile when she saw them hanging on to the sleek feathers for dear life.

She remembered how terrified she had been, clinging to the back of a bird before she learned how to fly!

'Hang on, what's that?' said Bimi suddenly.

A crowd of fairies were hovering in the air, jostling together as they fought to see something hanging on the wall.

'Let's go and see!' said Twink.

They struggled their way into the crowd, and saw a notice written on a large oak leaf:

Are you a fast flier?
Would you like to play for your school?
Then come to the
FLEDGE TRY-OUTS TOMORROW!
Fledge field after lessons.
Really good fliers only, please!
Madge Woodwing, Games Fairy

One of the older students laughed. 'Poor Madge – she still hasn't got over Glitterwings losing the Fairy Finals last year. She's determined to put together the best Fledge team ever.'

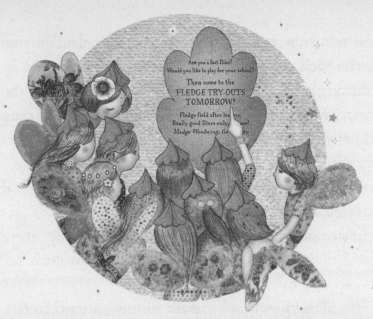

Are you a fast flier?
Would you like to play for your school?

Then come to the
FLEDGE TRY-OUTS
TOMORROW!

Fledge field after lessons.
Really good fliers only, please!
Madge Woodwing, Games Fairy

Twink stared at the notice. She had never played
Fledge before, but she loved watching the high-
speed game. It was probably a daft idea, but – but
maybe . . .

Bimi clutched Twink's arm. 'Twink, you should
try out!'

Trust Bimi to know what she was thinking! Twink
looked at the notice again, and sighed. 'I'm not a
good enough flier, Bimi. I'd get laughed off the
field.'

Bimi drew her away from the crowd. The two fairies flew slowly along, drifting downwards past empty classrooms. 'You would not! You won the award for best flier in the entire school last year, didn't you?'

Twink rolled her eyes. 'That was only because I had just learned how! It doesn't mean I'm good enough to play Fledge.'

'You should do it,' said Bimi. 'You really are a good flier, Twink. And the worst they can do is say no, so why not?'

Twink hesitated as a flutter of hope stirred in her. 'I don't know,' she said finally. 'I'll think about it.'

The Great Branch was the largest branch in the school – a long, high space with gracefully arched windows. Bright glow-worm lanterns hung from the ceiling, and rows of mossy tables were lined up and down its gleaming wooden floors, with a different-coloured flower hanging over each one.

Twink let out a contented breath as she flew in with the other Peony Branch fairies. Last term, she had thought the Great Branch looked like a garden at midnight, shadowy and mysterious. Now, in the pure, clear light of springtime, it looked like a garden at dawn.

'There we are!' she said, pointing to a table with a large pink peony over it. 'We're much nearer the back this year, aren't we?'

'That's because we're not little First Years any more – they don't need to keep such a close eye on us,' grinned Pix, a clever red-headed fairy.

The girls perched on their spotted mushroom seats, watching as the rest of the school flitted in. Twink glanced across at the Daffodil Branch table. The fairies sitting at it all looked terrified!

When everyone was finally seated, Miss Shimmery, the HeadFairy, lifted up from the platform at the front of the Branch. The school fell expectantly silent as she hovered above them, her rainbow wings gleaming.

'Welcome back!' she announced in her low, rich voice. 'And to all of our new students, a warm welcome.' She smiled down at the front row of tables. 'We hope you'll be very happy here at Glitterwings Academy.'

Miss Shimmery went on to make the usual announcements: they'd be expected to wear their uniforms from tomorrow, Flight lessons for the First Years would begin the next morning, no high-speed flying allowed in the corridors . . .

Twink looked out of the window. She couldn't see the Fledge field from here, but she could picture it in her mind – a circle of grass with a forest of different-sized poles rising up from it. Each pole had a hole through it, and when they played, the fairies jetted through them at speeds that would make your wings sizzle. It was such an exciting game! Should she *really* try out, though? Her neck prickled at the thought.

'Twink!' hissed Bimi, nudging her hard. 'Stand up, it's the school song.'

'Oh!' Twink jumped to her feet. She hadn't even noticed that the cricket band had started up! Hastily, she began to sing with the others:

Oh, Glitterwings, dear Glitterwings
Beloved oak tree scho-ool.
Good fairy fun for everyone,
That is our fairy ru-ule.
Our teachers wise,
Their magic strong,
With all our friends,
We can't go wrong.
Oh, Glitterwings, dear Glitterwings
Beloved oak tree scho-ool.

The music ended, and Miss Shimmery raised her arm in the air. 'Butterflies commence!'

A stream of brightly coloured butterflies floated into the branch, carrying oak-leaf platters piled high with food. The First Years gasped with delight. A blue and green butterfly dropped a platter of honey cakes on to the Peony Branch table, and another delivered acorn pitchers filled with fresh dew.

'New term, same old honey cakes,' said Sooze, drizzling nectar over hers from an almond-shell pitcher.

'I like honey cakes!' protested Sili, an excitable fairy with silver hair. 'And anyway, isn't it glimmery to be Second Years now? I feel so *grown-up*! Zena, don't I seem more grown-up to you?' Sili struck a pose.

'Oh, definitely,' laughed Zena. 'No one would ever guess that you're really a total wasp brain.'

As Sili squealed with pretended outrage, Bimi offered Twink a honey cake. 'You were miles away a moment ago!'

Twink glanced at the others. They were still chatting loudly, not paying any attention. 'I suppose I was thinking about the try-outs tomorrow,' she admitted.

'Well, you know what *I* think.' Bimi's blue eyes sparkled.

'How were your hols, you two?' asked Pix, leaning across the table.

Twink was relieved to change the subject, but later, as they were getting ready for bed, she whispered, 'Bimi, do you really think I should try out for Fledge?'

Bimi's blue head popped out of her soft cobweb

nightgown. 'Absolutely!' she whispered back. 'Do it, Twink!'

Twink hesitated. 'Maybe,' she said finally.

Nestling down into her moss bed, Twink pulled her petal duvet snugly around her. There was a window open, and the peony over her bed swayed slightly in the breeze. The inside of the flower was a soft, gentle pink, with bright yellow stamens curling at its centre.

Mrs Hover, the matron, bustled heavily up and down the branch. 'All right, girls, lights out!' The glow-worms faded, so that the only light was the moonlight angling into the branch.

'Goodnight, Twink,' whispered Bimi.

'Goodnight,' said Twink softly. It had been a long day, but even so she lay awake for a long time, gazing out of the moonlit window at the large, rustling oak leaves beyond.

Was she *really* a good enough flier to play Fledge?

Chapter Two

'Rise and shine, my lovelies!' In what seemed no time at all, Mrs Hover was back again, shaking a sleepy shoulder here and there. 'Come along now, flitter-flutter. It's a new term today!'

Twink opened her eyes. Sunshine flooded the branch, so that the peonies over each bed seemed to sparkle. How pretty! She sat up and yawned, smoothing her sleep-crumpled wings.

Mrs Hover appeared at her bedside, her ample arms full of still more peonies, in every shade of pink imaginable. 'Now then, my dear, shall we get your new uniform fitted?'

'Yes, please!' Twink bounced out of bed. She looked forward to this each new term.

Mrs Hover chose a bright pink flower and held it in front of Twink. 'Very nice. Goes with your hair a treat!'

Reaching into the petal pouch at her hip, Mrs Hover took out a pinch of fairy dust and threw it over the flower. There was a tinkling sound like tiny chimes, and suddenly Mrs Hover was holding a peony dress just Twink's size, with stripy sleeves and a fluttery petal skirt. A bright blue petal sash completed the picture, blue being the second-year colour.

'Glimmery!' said Twink happily. 'Thanks, Mrs Hover.'

Bimi's new uniform was bright pink like Twink's, and her blue hair gleamed against it like a river of bluebells. 'It's even nicer than last year's, isn't it?' she said.

'It's perfect!' Twink twirled in place, admiring her skirt. Then she popped her oak-leaf cap on to her head. 'There you go – I'm ready for the new term!'

When Mrs Hover had finished with the uniforms, she stood in the middle of the branch. 'Right! Who wants timetables?'

Twink clustered about with the others as Mrs Hover passed out the rose-petal timetables. She scanned her new classes eagerly.

Creature Kindness Continued: Amphibians and Reptiles. Flower Power II: An Introduction to Trees. Fairy Dust: Theory and Practice. Introduction to Weather Magic. Dance II.

'Weather Magic – now *that* sounds glimmery.' Sooze fluttered her wings with satisfaction. 'And no more Flight lessons, hurrah!'

Twink grinned to herself. She had rather liked their Flight lessons with gruff Mrs Lightwing, but Sooze had been wild with impatience after the first term. Only first-year babies took Flight!

'And look at all the free time we have,' commented Bimi. 'Hours and hours of it!'

Mrs Hover's plump face beamed. 'That's right – you'll be expected to take part in some sort of club or sport, now that you know your way around the school. Not to mention all the extra homework you'll have!'

Gazing at the free periods on her timetable, an image of herself zooming about the Fledge field popped into Twink's mind. She knew it was daft to even imagine it could happen, but – oh, it would be so ultra-glimmery to be on the team!

Bimi nudged her. 'Well?' she whispered.

Twink took a deep breath. 'OK,' she whispered back. 'I'll try out!'

When lessons finally ended that afternoon, Twink flew out to the Fledge field and hovered at its edge.

A dozen or so older fairies were already on the field, practising their moves. Twink's resolve wavered as she watched a fourth-year girl jet through a post hole so fast that her blue hair whistled behind her. They were all fantastic fliers!

'What are *you* doing here?' sneered a voice. 'It's for good fliers only, or didn't you read the notice!'

Twink glanced around and groaned to herself.

Hanging in the air beside her was the last fairy she wanted to see.

'None of your business, Mariella,' she said.

'You're not actually thinking of trying out!' Mariella burst out laughing.

Twink's wings stiffened as she glared at her. 'What's so funny?'

Mariella's eyes shone smugly. She flicked her silvery-green hair back. 'Well, I'm sure Madge won't want novice fliers like *you* on the team! What if you had trouble flying again and ruined a game for everyone?'

A chill clutched Twink's wings as she remembered the problems with flying she'd had her very first term. Could Mariella be right? *Don't be daft,* she reassured herself. *That was ages ago!*

'Well, I'm trying out anyway,' she said shortly.

'I *really* wouldn't bother if I were you –' started Mariella. Then she looked upwards, and a sudden smile burst across her face. 'Oh, I'm so excited! Aren't you? I can hardly wait to play!'

Twink stared at her in confusion. Before she could

The Fledge field

reply, a voice boomed, 'Here to try out, are you?'

Hovering just above them was a tall, solid fairy with dark green hair and wings. Twink's eyes widened as she recognised Madge Woodwing, the Games Fairy. The fifth-year girl was larger than any fairy Twink had ever seen, and looked as powerful as a small hawk.

Mariella nodded eagerly. 'Oh, yes! We were just talking about it, weren't we, Twink?'

No wonder Mariella had suddenly become so nice! 'Um – yes, that's right,' mumbled Twink.

'Good!' Madge clapped her large hands together. 'We've just finished the warm-up, but we're about to start a practice game if you want to join in.'

Twink gulped. The Games Fairy was obviously trying to be kind, but there was something a bit fierce about her. 'I – I *think* I want to try out, but I've never played Fledge before,' she admitted in a rush.

'Even better!' said Madge with a sudden grin. 'If you're a good flier I can train you up myself, and not have to break you of any bad habits. Do you know the rules?'

'Sort of,' said Twink. Her cheeks reddened. Oh, *why* did Mariella have to be there?

'Well, I'll just go over them for you. First, there's the Flea – that's him over there, sitting on the centre post. He won't sit still for long, though, once the game starts! He jumps about like a wild thing.' Madge gave the Flea an affectionate look.

Twink glanced apprehensively at the crouching

insect. He was combing his whiskers with his front legs, looking completely unconcerned.

Madge went on, 'The Flea's the whole object of the game – depending on what team you're on, you're either guarding him or stealing him. When you're playing with the Guards, there's only three of you, but when you're a Stealer, you've got six players. Right?'

'Um – right!' said Twink quickly. She could see Mariella smirking out of the corner of her eye.

'Now, if the Stealers gain possession of the Flea three times during a game, then the Guards lose. And at the same time, the Guards are trying to tag the Stealers. If they tag all six before they lose the Flea, *they* win. And that's all there is to it!' finished Madge with a grin. 'Got it?'

'I – I think so,' said Twink, hoping that the Games Fairy wasn't going to ask her to repeat any of that! She looked at the Flea again, and tried to hold back a shudder as she imagined tackling the spiky, hairy insect. 'But, um . . . catching the Flea . . . I mean . . .'

'Doesn't hurt him at all!' boomed Madge. 'He loves it! Right, off you go, then. You can both be Stealers. Mind you don't let the Guards tag you!'

That's not quite what I meant! thought Twink. Feeling hot and self-conscious, she flew towards the playing field.

Mariella skimmed quickly ahead of her. As they joined the other Stealers, she kept well away from Twink, hovering with her nose in the air. 'Good!' muttered Twink. Worrying about Mariella was the last thing she needed right now.

At the centre of the field, the three Guards clustered about the Flea. The little insect still sat preening himself, stroking his long, whiskery legs over his face. The blue-haired Fourth Year whom Twink had noticed before nudged her arm.

'You have to watch him like a cat!' she whispered. 'He's always leaping off when you least expect it.'

Twink nodded, grateful for the advice.

'And use the posts,' urged the girl. 'You can hide behind them to keep from being tagged, or zoom through one of the holes to shake a Guard off. But be careful – you can crash right into them if you're not looking.'

Suddenly she stuck her hand out with a grin. 'I'm Mia, by the way. Good luck!'

Madge blew a reed whistle, and the game started. 'Watch the Flea!' called someone. Just as Madge had said, the tiny insect was now jumping madly from post to post, soaring almost a foot in the air with each leap.

Twink darted towards him – and then zipped hastily away again as one of the Guards flew straight at her. Remembering Mia's advice about the posts, she did a quick midair somersault and dived through a hole.

'Good move!' called one of the other Stealers.

Twink grinned, but there was no time to savour her triumph. The game continued at a rocketing pace, each moment more exhilarating than the last. Everyone played hard and fast – and Twink had to admit that Mariella got some glimmery moves in. She really was a very good flyer, even if she was Twink's least favourite fairy in the world!

Finally, with three of their teammates tagged, the Stealers had caught the Flea twice. Once more, and they'd win.

Hovering behind a post, Twink peeked out. The Flea was on the move again! She forgot all about her dread of touching him. She had to catch him! She zoomed out of hiding as he sprang over her head, her fingers straining.

All at once a Guard spotted her. 'Oh, no you don't!' she called.

Twink gulped as the larger fairy barrelled towards her, and ducked out of the way just in time.

'Agh!' cried the Guard. Flying too fast to stop, she only barely missed crashing into a post. Her wings beat frantically as she tumbled through the air.

Now! Twink turned sharply and dived again, keeping her eyes on the Flea. Mariella was jetting towards him from the other direction, a determined grimace on her face.

But Twink got there first. Ignoring the Guard's angry shout, she scooped the Flea into her arms. He wriggled in her grasp, not spiky at all. His hairy legs

tickled like little feathers.

She had done it! They'd won! Excitement burst through Twink like fizzy dew as her teammates crowded around her, shouting congratulations and thumping her on the back.

'I can't believe it!' she gasped.

'Well done!' cried Mia. 'You're a natural!'

'Yes, well done, Twink,' simpered Mariella with a phoney smile. 'That was *so* clever of you.'

Suddenly Madge was there, beaming all across her broad face. 'Not bad,' she said, taking the Flea from Twink. Her green wings beat the air with strong, solid strokes. 'Good game, everyone – thanks for coming. I'll post the new team list after dinner.'

Chapter Three

Dinner that night seemed to last for ever. Twink nibbled at her seed cake, hardly tasting it. Oh, *where* was Madge? For the hundredth time, she twisted on her mushroom seat, peering at the upper-year tables.

Bimi touched her arm. 'You'll make the team, don't worry,' she whispered. 'That last move that you did was completely glimmery!'

Twink gave her best friend a grateful smile. Bimi had watched the try-outs without Twink knowing, and had been there to hug her excitedly as she flew off the field.

'Do you really think so?' she whispered back. 'Mariella played well too, Bimi, you know she did.'

Bimi shook her blue head. 'Not as well as you. Honestly, Twink – you don't have anything to worry about!'

Twink glanced down the table. Mariella was loudly telling a wide-eyed Lola all about the game, making the most of her every wing stroke.

'It was really the best move in the game, even if I do say so myself. Why, one of the older girls said to me that she's never *seen* a barrel roll done that way before! I'm sure Madge must have noticed it, too.' Mariella sat back smugly on her mushroom.

'Ooh, a barrel roll!' Sooze's violet eyes were wide and innocent. 'That's much better than winning the game – you'd better look out, Twink!'

Mariella scowled at her as the table burst into laughter.

'Twink, *look*! She's putting the team lists up!' squealed Sili.

Twink whipped about on her seat. Yes, there was Madge down at the end of the Great Branch,

tacking a rose petal to the wall!

'Come on, Bimi!' she cried. Leaving their seats, she and Bimi flew hurriedly down the length of the Branch. Mariella and Lola followed close behind.

A small crowd of fairies was already clustered about the notice. 'Well done, Pip!' said an older fairy to her friend. 'I knew you'd make it.'

Twink lifted up in the air, straining to see. There was the list! She scanned it quickly, holding her breath. Where was her name? Surely it had to be there!

But it wasn't.

Twink's cheeks blazed with embarrassment as she sank back down to the ground. 'I – I suppose I wasn't good enough after all,' she muttered to Bimi. And she had been so certain! At least Mariella wasn't on the list, either. That really would have been too much to bear.

But Bimi was still looking at the list. 'Wait – there you are, down at the bottom!' she said, clutching Twink's arm. Twink shot up in the air again, her pulse pounding. And there it was:

Team reserves: Twink Flutterby, Second Year
Mariella Gossamer, Second Year

Team reserve? With *Mariella*? Twink stared at their names, battling mixed feelings. On the one wing, it was great to be on the team at all . . . but on the other wing, being a reserve with Mariella wasn't exactly what she had hoped for!

'*Reserve?*' shrieked a voice. Hovering a few fairies away, Mariella looked like she had just swallowed a gnat.

'But that's not fair!' squeaked Lola. 'You're a much better player than that.'

An older girl in a bluebell dress frowned. 'You're lucky to be on the team at all,' she pointed out. 'There's plenty who'd be happy to be a reserve if *you* aren't!'

Mariella seemed to choke on her reply. 'No, I'm happy to be a reserve,' she muttered, glaring across at Twink as if it were her fault. 'I was just . . . surprised, that's all.'

Madge appeared, her large green wings stirring the air. 'Glad to hear it!' she boomed. 'You're both good players, but you're still very young. I need you to prove to me that you've got what it takes, and if you do, I'll make you both full Fledge players next year.'

Next year! Twink tried to smile. 'Yes, OK,' she said.

'Glimmery!' said Mariella, looking as if she really

meant it. But the moment Madge flew off, her smile faded. The two fairies looked at each other as the crowd around the notice drifted away.

'Um . . . well, congratulations,' said Twink awkwardly. 'To us both, I mean. I suppose we did well to get on the team at all.'

'Speak for yourself!' snapped Mariella. She skimmed off without another word, with Lola flapping along after her.

Bimi grimaced. 'Poor you, having to play with her! But Twink, at least you're on the team. That's the main thing.'

Twink nodded. 'I know. I'll just have to keep telling myself that!'

But in the weeks that followed, Madge kept them so busy practising that Mariella didn't have time to be unpleasant. The team flew almost every day, working out glimmery new moves and zooming through the wooden posts like comets. Twink loved every moment of it – even the way her muscles ached at the end of a hard game.

'All right, listen up!' called Madge at the start of practice one day. 'Our first match is this Saturday. We're playing against Sparklelight Academy, and you know what *that* means!'

Twink glanced at the fairies hovering around her. They were all nodding seriously, even Mariella. Twink raised her hand.

'Yes?' barked Madge.

'Er – what does it mean?' asked Twink shyly.

Madge's mouth dropped open. 'What does it *mean*? Why, Sparklelight is practically the best team in the whole league! We have to beat them at least twice this season, or we won't get into the finals.'

Twink swallowed. 'Oh.'

'And we've only got three matches with them altogether – so this one is very important,' said Madge sternly. 'Now out on the field, everyone! Let's make this our best practice yet.'

The practice game started, with Twink on the Guards team. The Flea was in a mischievous mood, bounding gleefully from post to post. In no time at all, it was a wild, frenzied game, with the Guards racing about after the Flea and the Stealers darting in from all directions, trying to grab him.

'Oh, stay *still*,' panted Twink. The Flea landed nimbly on one of the posts, jumped up and down a few times, and then bounded off again. Argh! Twink dived through the air after him, with a pair of Stealers twisting quickly out of her way.

Crack! The sound echoed across the field. Whirling about midair, Twink saw that a fourth-year fairy called Vera had crashed into a post. She fell to the ground in what seemed like slow motion.

Her heart pounding, Twink swooped down after her. The team landed about Vera in a cluster. 'Are you all right?' asked Mia, gripping her shoulder.

Vera's face was flushed and damp. 'Oh, it's my stupid wing! I wasn't looking where I was going, and now I think I've broken it!'

Madge appeared and crouched down beside the injured fairy, feeling her wing. 'You've broken it, all right,' she said grimly. 'Come on, let's get you to the infirmary. Mia, give me a hand.' Lifting Vera up between them, they slowly flew her off the field.

Twink hugged herself as she watched them head towards the tree. Fledge was such an exhilarating game, but it was awful when something like this happened!

The team broke into smaller groups, murmuring worriedly about Vera. Mariella flitted over beside Twink. 'Well, you know what *this* means,' she said.

Twink shook her head. 'No, what?'

The pointy-faced fairy let out an impatient breath. 'Honestly, Twink! Vera's not going to be playing in the Sparklelight match, is she? So one of us will be.'

A thrill darted across Twink's wings as she realised Mariella was right. She would never have wanted Vera to get injured, but — but oh, it *would* be wonderful to actually play in the match, instead of just hanging about on the sidelines!

'But I wouldn't get your hopes up, if I were you,' smirked Mariella. 'Madge is sure to choose the *best* player.' She jetted off across the field.

Twink grimaced after her. She knew she had a chance, no matter what Mariella said!

Finally Madge and Mia reappeared, flying down the hill to the field.

'Is Vera all right?' asked a fifth-year student anxiously.

The Games Fairy sighed. 'Fine, but she won't be playing for a few weeks — her wing's got a nasty break.' She narrowed her eyes at Twink and Mariella, and then gave a decisive nod. 'Twink, I want you to play in the Sparklelight match in her place.'

Twink caught her breath as the rest of the team grinned at her. 'Oh, thank you!' she burst out, excitement pounding through her wings. 'I'll play really well, Madge, I promise.'

'I know,' said Madge with a sudden chuckle. 'Because you'll have *me* to answer to otherwise.'

Twink smiled happily – though somehow she didn't think Madge was really joking!

Madge swooped to the ground and picked up a pile of bright yellow petal pads. She handed them out, slapping one into each girl's hand. 'These are your strategy books! I've worked out some glimmery set pieces for the Sparklelight match, and I want you all to memorise them. Sparklelight won't even know what's hit them!'

'What about me?' asked Mariella, just managing to keep the sour note out of her voice.

'You too, Mariella – just in case!' Madge handed Mariella a yellow petal pad as well.

Flipping through her strategy book, Twink's excitement started to feel more like apprehension. The set pieces all had titles like: *Guarding the Flea* –

a Double Bluff, and *Super Triple Fake-Out Using the Centre Post.* Pages and pages of instructions for each of them! How would she ever remember all of this by Saturday?

Twink saw Mariella watching her with narrowed eyes. She quickly closed the petal pad, trying to look unconcerned. *I'll just have to study extra hard, that's all,* she decided. *I've got to do well in the match – I've just got to!*

Chapter Four

'Weather magic is the most *dramatic* of all fairy magic,' intoned Mrs Starbright. Her blue sleeves billowed as she raised her arms. 'We are responsible for making snowflakes! Rainbows! Thunderstorms!'

Mariella stifled a yawn. This was the most boring class ever. Who cared about making snowflakes or rainbows? She'd rather do something important – something that would get her *noticed*.

'We are also responsible for shooting stars,' continued Mrs Starbright, adjusting her cobweb shawl. 'Who knows why we must help stars fall from the sky? Yes, Pix?'

'Stars are very hard-working,' said Pix eagerly. 'They'll keep burning for ever, even if they're exhausted, until a fairy tells them they can stop.'

'Perfect!' cried Mrs Starbright. 'And then once they've fallen, their star dust makes a new star – such a beautiful cycle. Now, who read ahead in their petal books to find out *how* we make stars fall?'

Pix's hand shot in the air again. 'If you find a star that looks weak and tired, you just concentrate on it

Mrs Starbright

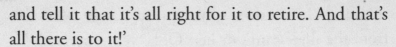

and tell it that it's all right for it to retire. And that's all there is to it!'

'Yes!' Mrs Starbright gave a rapturous sigh. 'Shooting stars could not be simpler.'

Mariella rolled her eyes as the lecture went on. That Pix was such a show-off. Mariella didn't know why the others couldn't see how insufferable she was. Of course, they were all pretty insufferable, too!

Especially Twink. Mariella propped her chin on her hand, brooding to herself. It had been bad enough when Twink made the team, but how could Madge have chosen her over Mariella for the Sparklelight match? It was so unfair! Mariella knew that *she'd* be the star player if only Twink wasn't around.

She slid a glance towards Twink. She sat with her forehead furrowed, studying her strategy book from under her arm.

Mariella held back a groan. Twink had been studying practically non-stop for days now! At this rate, she'd know all the set pieces inside and out, and fly brilliantly in the match.

Unless . . . a slow smile spread across Mariella's face as a plan came to her. Ooh, yes – perfect! *Ha ha, Twink,* she thought smugly. The pink-haired fairy wasn't going to play quite as well in the match as she thought. Then Madge would see what a wasp brain she'd been not to choose Mariella – and with any luck, she'd be so furious that she'd throw Twink off the team for good!

The day before the match the Fledge team practised for hours, chasing the Flea and hurtling around the posts until their wings were aching.

'That's it!' called Madge finally. She hovered in the air, looking pleased. 'Excellent practice, everyone. I think we have a real chance of beating Sparklelight tomorrow.'

'It'll be the first time in years if we do,' whispered Mia to Twink. 'But I hope Madge is right!'

'Now listen up,' continued Madge. 'We leave for Sparklelight straight after breakfast tomorrow, and I want you all to get a good night's sleep tonight. No staying up late, no larking about.

You're to REST! Understand?'

Twink nodded agreement with the others. She was so tired already, she couldn't imagine doing anything but falling into bed tonight!

'Good,' said Madge with a sudden smile. 'Go on then, get your showers!'

Twink flitted back to the changing log with the others. After a soothing rainwater shower, she pulled on her peony dress, tying her blue sash around her waist.

Mariella appeared beside her, patting her silvery-green hair dry with a bit of spongy moss. 'Looking forward to the match tomorrow?'

Twink looked up in surprise. 'Oh – yes!' she said. 'It'll be fun to see another school. Mia says the hosting school always throws a party for the visiting team – it'll be really glimmery.'

The most glimmery part of all would be playing in the match, she thought, though it didn't seem very tactful to mention it!

Mariella looked like she was thinking the same thing. 'Mmm. I suppose. I almost went to

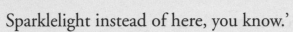

Sparklelight instead of here, you know.'

Twink paused as she pulled on her dark pink pixie boots. 'You did?'

Mariella nodded, combing her hair out with a thistle comb. 'Mummy says you get a much better class of fairy at Sparklelight, but my father put his wing down. He said he wasn't going to have me turn out a snob.' She wrinkled her nose. 'It was *so* unfair of him! Mummy went to Sparklelight, and loved it.'

Privately, Twink thought Mariella's father had a point – no one was more stuck-up than Mariella already! But she didn't say this out loud. 'Oh,' she murmured. 'That's too bad.'

Mariella lifted a shoulder, looking almost friendly for a change. 'Well, never mind about that. Have you memorised all the set pieces?'

Twink hesitated. 'I *think* so. There's so many of them, but –' She stopped at the look of wide-eyed horror on Mariella's face.

'You *think*?' she echoed.

Twink licked her lips, suddenly uncomfortable. 'Well – yes. I mean, we've gone over most of them in practice, but there might be one or two that –'

Glancing over her shoulder, Mariella lowered her voice. 'Twink! Are you saying you *haven't* memorised them all?'

'No, I have!' cried Twink. 'Only – well, you know, there's so many of them, and they're all so long . . .' She trailed off. A moment ago she had been perfectly happy with how well she knew the set pieces, but suddenly she felt very unsure.

Mariella shook her head. 'Twink, you've got to learn them!' she hissed. 'You've got to know them inside and out before the match, or else Madge will never forgive you.'

Twink swallowed. 'Well – I was planning on going over them again tonight during evening study –'

Mariella's green eyes widened. 'But that's only an hour! And if you don't know them all . . .'

'But – that's all I can do,' faltered Twink. 'You know we're supposed to get a good night's sleep tonight –'

Mariella stared at Twink as if she couldn't believe

what she was hearing. 'Well, which is better, to be a bit tired and know all the set pieces, or wide awake and useless? It's your first match, Twink! Don't you want to show Madge you've got what it takes?'

'Of course!' cried Twink. 'But –'

Mariella huffed out a breath. 'Well, it's up to you, of course, but if *I* had been chosen for the match, I know what I'd do – I'd make sure I knew all the set pieces, no matter how late I had to stay up!'

Flinging her woven-grass towel over her shoulder, Mariella headed for her bark locker without another word. Twink stared after her, biting her lip. *It's all right,* she told herself. *I've been studying the set pieces for days now. I know them, I really do!*

But suddenly it was as though they'd all vanished from her head.

Secret Flea Manoeuvre. When I make an X with my wings, all Stealers are to fly to the centre of the field. When the Guards try to tag –

Twink stifled a yawn as she turned the page. Nestled beside her under the covers, the wooden

glow-worm lantern gave off a soft glow. The glow-worm inside it lay curled up grumpily, looking as tired as she felt.

'Just a few more,' Twink whispered to him. She yawned again, trying to stop the letters on the page from blurring together. If only her moss bed wasn't so lovely and soft!

'Twink?' murmured a sleepy voice. 'Are you still awake?'

Twink poked her head out from under the covers. Bimi was sitting up in the next bed, her blue hair tousled in the moonlight. 'What are you doing up?' she whispered. 'It's almost three o'clock.'

Twink swallowed. 'Just – going over the set pieces for tomorrow.'

'But you know them all already! Aren't you supposed to get a good night's sleep?'

Twink clutched her strategy book tightly. 'I've only got a few more to go over.'

'A few *more*?' Bimi's eyes widened. 'But, Twink –'

'Hush, you'll wake everyone up!' Twink glanced over her shoulder at the sleeping branch.

Bimi shook her head. 'I really think you should go to sleep now, Twink. You're going to be exhausted.'

Worn out with worry and lack of sleep, Twink felt her patience snap. 'Stop nagging!' she whispered sharply. 'I know what I'm doing, all right?'

A hurt frown crossed Bimi's face. 'Fine. But I think you're being completely daft. You already *know* all the set pieces!' She flipped over on to her side, pointedly opening her silver and gold wings to hide herself.

Twink felt like crying. Oh, that was just what she needed – a row with her best friend!

No time to worry about it now, though. She couldn't take a chance on not knowing the set pieces. Wiping her eyes, Twink burrowed back under her covers and started to read again, her eyes aching with the effort to stay open.

Awakened by angry whispers, Mariella had lain quietly in the darkness, listening to the argument with satisfaction. Oh, how funny! Twink had fallen for every word!

Now we'll see how well she plays tomorrow, she thought smugly. Lulled by the sound of turning pages coming from Twink's bed, Mariella drifted back to sleep, smiling to herself.

Chapter Five

'Go, Mia! Go, go!' shouted the Glitterwings cheering section. The twenty fairies who had accompanied the team to Sparklelight Academy sat on special mushrooms down at the front of the pitch, screaming and shouting, trying to make as much noise as they could.

Hovering in the air as she guarded the Flea, Twink saw blearily that Mia was chasing a Sparklelight Stealer. With a sudden dive, Mia tagged the Stealer with a flourish. The Glitterwings fairies cheered and beat their wings, waving oak-leaf banners.

Twink yawned behind her hand. Oh, she was so tired! The team had ridden to Sparklelight on a flock of grey and yellow tits, the school being too far away to fly to on their own. Twink had hardly been able to keep upright in her saddle.

Normally she would have loved travelling to a different school, especially one as grand as this. Sparklelight Academy was behind a waterfall in a woodland lake, with cosy caves for the classrooms and sleeping quarters.

The Sparklelight Fledge field was just as impressive, with the posts rising up out of a shallow forest pool that was just like a mirror. Reflections of the trees gleamed in the water. Twink could see how lovely it was, even if she was too sleepy to appreciate it.

At least I know all the set pieces, she thought. Which was a good thing, as Sparklelight had some pretty glimmery set pieces themselves! It had been a close, quick match so far. The Flea had been tagged twice already – but as Sparklelight only had one Stealer left, Glitterwings' victory seemed certain.

At the opposite end of the field, Mia and the other Guard were chasing the remaining Stealer. Twink hovered beside the Flea, relieved that it showed no signs of going anywhere.

Oh, hurry up and catch that last Stealer so we can win, she thought drowsily. *I want to go home and get some sleep!*

No, she had to keep alert! Fluttering in midair, Twink shook out her arms. But a moment later she was yawning again. It was so lovely and warm out here . . . her head drooped, and her eyes shut despite themselves. Slowly, she started drifting towards the ground.

'HURRAH!' screamed the Sparklelight students.

Twink jerked awake – and gasped with horror! The Sparklelight Stealer was hovering only a wing's length away, holding the struggling Flea triumphantly over her head. Twink gaped in confusion as the Sparklelight players all rushed into the air, embracing their teammate. But . . . how had they lost the match?

She flew in a daze to the lily-pad sidelines. The

rest of the Glitterwings team was there ahead of her, huddled together talking with their wings almost touching. They fell silent when Twink landed beside them. Mariella had her silvery eyebrows raised.

'What happened?' asked Twink nervously. 'I didn't see –'

The lily pad sloshed in the water as Madge landed. 'I'll tell you what happened! You fell asleep!' she boomed.

Twink gulped. 'I –'

'You were practically SNORING out there!' Madge's broad face was red with anger. 'I signalled for you to do a Single Swoop Move to catch that last Stealer, and you didn't even see me – she stole the Flea right out from under your nose! Twink, how *could* you?'

Oh, no! Twink's wings felt icy. 'I – I'm sorry,' she stammered. 'I didn't mean to –'

'Didn't you get enough sleep last night?' demanded Madge. 'You didn't, did you? And after what I told you!'

Twink's face burned. 'I'm sorry,' she whispered again.

'We could have won against Sparklelight,' raged Madge, punching her fist into her palm. 'We almost had it! Oh, you silly little girl!'

'But Madge, she was only up late because she was studying the set pieces!' put in Mariella, her eyes wide.

'Studying the *set pieces*?' Madge scowled thunderously at Twink. 'Didn't you KNOW them already?'

Twink winced. She wished Mariella hadn't said anything! 'I – I *thought* so, but – I just wanted to make sure,' she mumbled.

Madge glared at her for a moment, and then let out a heavy breath. 'Well, come on, everyone – let's go to the party,' she said wearily. 'We might as well *try* to enjoy ourselves.'

The Sparklelight party was held in a large cavern just behind the glittering fall of water, with bright patterns of light dancing on the walls. The food was delicious – cress cakes and fizzy dew and lily seeds –

but Twink could only pick at her share. She felt as if she might never eat again.

The rest of the Glitterwings team stood clustered together, talking in low voices. *Go and join them,* Twink told herself. *Say something!*

But how could she face them? It was all her fault that they had lost the game. She didn't even know if she was still on the team or not!

Suddenly Mariella appeared at her side. 'Are you all right?' she asked.

Twink looked up, startled. 'Er – yes, I suppose.'

Mariella's green eyes were large with concern. 'Well, I think Madge was very unfair, shouting at you like that in front of the whole team!'

Twink blinked. 'You . . . do?'

'Of course!' cried Mariella. 'Falling asleep could have happened to anyone. You were only trying to learn the set pieces.'

Twink gaped at her. Was this really Mariella? 'Um . . . thanks.' She glanced at the rest of the team, and tried to sound casual. 'What do the others think?'

Mariella made a face. 'Oh, you'd think they'd

never made a mistake in their lives, the way they're carrying on! Just ignore them, Twink.'

Twink's spirits plummeted. 'They're really cross with me, then?'

Mariella helped herself to a bit of Twink's cress cake. 'They'll get over it. Try not to worry, Twink. Just let them have their little strop!'

Twink risked another look at the team. They were all staring right at her, frowning and nudging each other. Oh, what were they *saying*? Was she still on the team or not?

Suddenly she couldn't bear the suspense any longer. 'I'm going to go and talk to Madge,' she said, and flitted off before Mariella could reply.

Her spirits sank as she approached Madge, who stood chatting with the Sparklelight Games Fairy. Twink hovered to one side, not at all sure how to word her question.

'Well, what is it?' demanded Madge gruffly, scowling down at her. The Sparklelight fairy tactfully chose that moment to flit off for another cress cake.

Twink's lavender wings trembled. 'I – I just wanted to say again how sorry I am.'

Madge sighed, and took a swig of fizzy dew. 'Well, we've got two more chances at Sparklelight. So we might beat them yet.'

Twink swallowed, and then blurted it out. 'And I was wondering – am I still on the team?'

Madge was silent for a long moment, considering her. Twink tried to stand up straight under the scrutiny. Her heart was drumming so hard that she was certain it must be echoing around them.

'I haven't decided,' said Madge, tapping a finger on her acorn cup. 'You're a good player, Twink – but that was a really silly stunt, sitting up half the night before a match!'

Twink's wings drooped. 'I know,' she whispered. Oh, what had she done! She loved being on the team, and now she might lose it for good, all because of her own stupidity.

'All right, I'll give you one more chance,' said Madge finally. 'But you're going to have to work hard to show me that you've got what it takes!'

Chapter
Six

The story of how the Sparklelight match had been lost travelled quickly about Glitterwings. Twink's pointed ears burned with the whispers and comments, until she wanted to crawl away into a knothole and hide.

'Ooh, be careful, girls,' cooed a third-year fairy to her friends the day after the game, as Peony Branch flew past them on their way to breakfast. 'Twink might not have got enough sleep last night – she could fall right out of the air on top of us!'

Twink whirled furiously about, but the older girls

were already gone, flitting away like bright, laughing birds. Suddenly Twink realised that Sooze was laughing, too! She stared at her friend in hurt amazement.

Pix poked Sooze in the ribs. 'Sooze, hush!' she hissed.

'I'm sorry!' gasped Sooze. She bounced in the air, clutching her sides. 'Oh, but Twink, it really is funny – you falling asleep, right out on the Fledge field –'

'It is *not* funny!' shouted Twink, her fists clenched.

Sooze's eyes widened. 'What are you so cross about? It's only a game, Twink!'

Hardly able to see for the tears, Twink flew away as fast as she could. Not the Great Branch! She couldn't bear to sit there with the whole school sniggering at her. Darting through the stream of fairies heading for breakfast, Twink jetted downwards towards the library.

The tall room was empty this early in the morning. Its narrow shelves touched the ceiling high overhead, and long windows let in the sunlight.

Swooping into the room, Twink perched on one of the spotted mushroom seats and drew her knees to her chest, burying her head in her arms. It was so unfair! *How* could Sooze laugh at her? What sort of a friend was she, anyway?

It's not her fault, said a little voice inside of her. *It's yours, for falling asleep!*

'Twink?'

She looked up. Bimi hovered in front of her, her expression worried. 'Are you all right?' she asked.

Twink shrugged and wiped her eyes. 'Oh, of course! Why shouldn't I be?'

Bimi sat down beside her, rubbing her silver and gold wing against Twink's lavender one. 'It was really mean of Sooze to laugh like that.'

'She's right, though,' said Twink bitterly. 'It *was* funny. Especially to the Sparklelight team! I really let everyone down, didn't I?'

Bimi looked uncomfortable. 'You didn't mean to. Besides, who knows . . . maybe you wouldn't have tagged the Stealer even if you had seen Madge's signal.'

'But that's the point – I didn't even see it!' burst out Twink. 'Madge won't ever trust me again. The whole team probably hates me!'

Bimi started to reply, and then stopped. 'Well . . . not getting any sleep *wasn't* the cleverest thing to do before a match,' she said finally, playing with her sash. 'But now you know better, so –'

'Oh, thanks a lot!' cried Twink, jumping up. 'You just couldn't let it drop, could you? You have to be so *right* all the time!'

Her voice echoed around the high, empty room. Deep down, Twink knew she was being unreasonable – none of this was Bimi's fault. But suddenly it didn't matter.

Bimi clapped her wings together in exasperation. 'Well, you *shouldn't* have stayed up so late! I know you were just worried about learning the set pieces, but –'

'But it's my fault that we lost – right?' Twink folded her arms over her chest as she hovered.

Bimi let out a breath. 'Oh, Twink, I don't want to argue! Can't we just –'

Twink didn't wait to hear the rest of it. She skimmed from the room as fast as she could, banging the heavy door shut behind her.

'Stay still, you wretched flea!' shouted Madge. But the insect was in a playful mood, jumping from post to post with wild abandon. Landing on the tallest, he waggled his antennae at Madge and then leapt away again as she swooped down on him, red-faced.

Twink and Mariella hovered at the edge of the field, watching as Madge tried to set up the practice game.

'Did . . . um . . . did the others say anything about me in the changing branch today?' whispered Twink to Mariella.

Her wings felt stiff as she waited for Mariella's answer. She had been keeping herself apart from the rest of the team ever since the Sparklelight match, too nervous of their reaction to risk talking to them.

The pointy-faced fairy shrugged. 'Nothing much. Don't worry about it.'

What did *nothing much* mean?

Twink bit her lip and glanced at the rest of the team, hovering a little way away.

'Ha – got you!' Madge grabbed the Flea and flew with him to the centre post, plunking him down into place. The Flea turned its back on her, looking sulky.

'But what did they actually say?' Twink whispered

as she and Mariella took their places. They were both playing on the Stealer team this game, hovering with the others in a circle around the Guards until Madge gave them the signal to begin.

Mariella gave her a troubled look. 'Well . . . it was just Mia. And a couple of the others.'

'Yes, but what did she *say*?' cried Twink in agony.

Mariella sighed. 'She said that you're an even worse player now than before. I *really* wouldn't pay any attention to her, Twink,' she added hastily. 'She's not worth your time!'

Twink swallowed hard, fighting tears. Had friendly, blue-haired Mia really said that? But she knew it must be true. By now the rest of the school seemed to have forgotten about the Sparklelight match, but the team still hadn't spoken to her, not once. She knew they must wish she had never made the team.

The two weeks since the match had felt very lonely to Twink. She'd apologised to Bimi after the incident in the library, but things hadn't really felt the same between them since. And because she was

still too angry with Sooze to be on good terms with her either, Twink had been spending a lot of time on her own. In fact, she spoke more to Mariella now than practically anyone else!

Madge blew her reed whistle, and the practice game started. The Flea took off from his post, the Guards hot on his heels. Pip, a fourth-year student with bright green hair, flitted past. Too late, Twink twisted in the air, trying to tag her – but her fingers closed over empty air.

Twink's wings burned. Everyone must be thinking that she couldn't play well even when she was awake! Keeping her eyes fixed determinedly on the Flea, Twink swooped around a post at top speed.

'Oof!' she cried as she collided with another fairy. She realised it was Mia, and wanted to sink into the ground.

Mia rubbed her wing with a grimace. 'Ouch! Are you –'

'Sorry,' mumbled Twink. She jetted quickly away, not waiting to hear Mia's response.

The rest of the game seemed a nightmare that would never end. Certain that the team must be sneering at her every wing stroke, Twink fumbled each move she tried. Finally, when she caught the Flea but then dropped him again, Madge blew her whistle piercingly.

Twink hovered, red-faced, as the Flea bounced nimbly away. Madge flew up and propped her hands on her hips, her large green wings stirring the air.

'What's up with you, Twink?' she demanded. 'You've been playing like you've got a bag over your head lately! Are you *still* not getting enough sleep?'

Twink winced and looked down, fiddling with the hem of her oak-leaf team uniform. She had been so proud the first time she put it on! Now it just seemed like a bad joke.

'I don't know,' she said. 'I just . . . feel sort of nervous.'

Madge sighed. 'Well, I gave you another chance, but it's not working out, is it?'

Twink felt as if Madge had dunked her in an icy pond. 'What do you mean?' she stammered.

'I mean you're off the team!' snapped Madge. 'You're going to have to try out for me again before I'll let you back on – and I'll only hold your place for a couple of weeks, so you'd better get your act together quickly!'

Twink saw Mia and the others glance at each other, and struggled to hold back tears. 'But – but what about the Forestglow match this Saturday?' she whispered. 'Vera's still out with her wing –'

Madge shook her head. 'Sorry, Twink, but I can't

depend on you, not the way you've been playing. You're off, I said – now go on, flap off!'

Back in the changing branch, Twink showered and changed as quickly as she could, desperate to be away before practice was over and the rest of the team came in. She could hardly blame Madge, she supposed – but oh, how humiliating! And after everything the team had been saying about her, too!

Twink's fingers trembled as she tied her sash about her waist. Clapping her oak-leaf cap on to her head, she grabbed up her petal bag and started to skim from the branch.

'Oh!' She fluttered backwards as Mariella flew in. Her cheeks caught fire. 'I've got to go,' she muttered, and tried to push past the other fairy.

'Twink, wait!' Mariella grabbed her arm and pulled her into one of the bark partitions, banging the door shut behind them. 'Listen, I've got an idea,' she whispered.

'Didn't you hear Madge?' Twink choked out. 'I'm off the team! And – and Mia and everyone else must

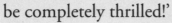

be completely thrilled!'

Mariella shook her silvery-green head as the other fairies started fluttering in. 'Who cares what they think?' she hissed. 'Didn't *you* hear Madge? All you've got to do is try out for her again, and you're back on the team!'

Twink shrugged, trying to hold back tears. 'I know – but –'

'And *I'm* going to help you do it,' continued Mariella. 'We'll practise like mad until you get your confidence back!'

Twink felt her mouth fall open. She snapped it shut again. 'You – you want to help me practise? But why?'

Mariella gave her an earnest nudge. 'Because I want to help, that's why! Come on, Twink – we're on the team together. Why *wouldn't* I want to help you?'

Twink stared at her in amazement. Mariella, offering to help? But then again . . . why not? She had been nice these last few weeks – and so sympathetic over how the rest of the team were treating

Twink! There was really no reason for Twink not to trust her.

'I . . . yes, all right!' said Twink. She managed a wavering smile. 'Thanks, Mariella.'

'That's more like it,' grinned Mariella. 'Don't worry, Twink – we'll have you back on the team in no time!'

Chapter Seven

'So, ah . . . springtime is a very busy time,' mumbled Mr Woodleaf, peering nervously at his class. 'Creatures such as . . . er . . . amphibians, especially, depend on us.'

Twink sighed. Another year with Mr Woodleaf in Creature Kindness, and he seemed just as terrified of them as ever!

Propping her chin on her hand, she gazed out of the window towards the Fledge field. Her wings tingled at the thought of zooming about the posts with the team again. And maybe it wouldn't be too much longer before she could.

She looked across the branch to where Mariella sat whispering with Lola. Who would ever have thought that the pointy-faced fairy would be so helpful? But true to her word, Mariella had been practising with Twink every afternoon for days now, going over and over the moves with her. Twink could feel her confidence flooding back. Why, she might even be back on the team in time for the Forestglow match tomorrow!

Twink started as Mr Woodleaf heaved a large walnut bucket full of water on to his mushroom desk. *What* was he doing? She and Bimi exchanged perplexed glances.

Mr Woodleaf ran a hand through his dark green hair. 'Right, ah . . . I have a very worried tadpole here.'

A tadpole! The class stood up, craning to see. Twink's eyes widened as she spotted a large, dark shape swimming about inside the bucket, with a long tail flicking behind it.

Mr Woodleaf cleared his throat. 'You see, ah . . .

tadpoles don't always want to become frogs.'

Reaching into the bucket, he gently lifted the tadpole partly out of the water. The class *oohed* in sympathy as they saw the wide-eyed expression on the little creature's face. It looked completely petrified!

Mr Woodleaf set the tadpole free again, and it hurriedly dived back under the water. Mr Woodleaf gloomily wiped his hands on a bit of mossy sponge.

'He feels safe in the water, you see. We have to help him want to be a frog, or else he'll stay stuck as a tadpole for ever.'

Pix's hand flew up into the air. 'Sir, should we sing him a song, like the frightened ladybirds we helped back in the first year?'

Mr Woodleaf nodded. 'Yes, but a very different sort of song. Frogs do their own singing, you see – so to make him want to be a frog, we need to, ah . . . croon to him in his own language.'

Throwing his head back, Mr Woodleaf let out a loud, '*Ribbit! Croak-croak-ribbity-ribbit!*'

Twink burst out laughing before she could stop

herself – but it didn't matter, as everyone else was laughing as well!

Mr Woodleaf's cheeks reddened. 'Ah . . . yes, well . . . let's hear *you* all do it. If we can make him want to be a frog, then our magic will speed up the transformation for him. All together, now! Try to follow the tune.'

Stifling her giggles, Twink struggled to master the ribbiting sounds. They were harder than she'd thought! Soon the Creature Kindness branch was

Mr Woodleaf

echoing with ribbits and croaks. Mr Woodleaf conducted them with his hands, humming under his breath.

In the bucket, a rippling appeared on the surface of the water. A dark, round head peeked up over the rim.

'Keep singing!' hissed Mr Woodleaf, still waving his hands about madly.

Her eyes glued to the tadpole, Twink croaked and ribbited louder than ever. The little creature blinked at them. A broad smile appeared across its face as it swished its tail about.

Then all at once, the tadpole began to grow a pair of hind legs. And then a pair of front legs grew, and the long tail began to shrink! Twink gasped as the tadpole's gills disappeared. Catching herself, she started to sing again.

With a splash, the tadpole leapt out of the bucket and squatted, dripping, on the desk. As the fairies sang with all their might, its skin changed from glossy black to bright green. Its eyes widened and turned gold. Finally the transformation was

complete. It was a baby frog!

The girls stopped singing and cheered, beating their wings together. As the magpie's call pierced through the school, signalling the end of lessons, Mr Woodleaf picked up the frog with a shy, pleased smile.

'Well done, girls! Ah . . . your homework tonight is to write a report about how to change tadpoles into frogs. Don't forget to include the tune!'

Twink quickly gathered up her books, humming to herself. Creature Kindness was their last lesson of the day. She could hardly wait to get on to the Fledge field again!

'Another practice with Mariella?' asked Bimi casually, not looking at her.

Twink nodded. 'That's right.'

'Oh,' said Bimi, lifting a wing.

Twink hesitated with a petal book in her hand, not sure what to say next. Bimi had been acting funny about her practice sessions for days now. 'What's wrong?' she asked finally.

Bimi made a face, flapping her bright wings. 'Oh,

I don't know! It's just strange that Mariella's being so nice, that's all.'

Twink shook her head as the others started flitting from the branch. 'I know, but Mariella's different when we play Fledge. Honestly, Bimi, she's helped me loads already! We've spent hours and hours practising together.'

'Mmm. And what is *she* getting out of it?' Bimi drew her blue eyebrows together sceptically.

Twink let out a breath. Oh! Bimi was acting so *right* again. It was just like when she had told Twink to go to sleep instead of studying the set pieces for the match! She shoved the petal book into her bag.

'We're both on the team, that's all,' she said stiffly. 'Teammates help each other – I wouldn't expect you to understand!'

The Flea leapt from post to post, sailing high in the air with every jump. Twink narrowed her eyes as she swooped after it. Timing her attack just right, she twisted to change direction – and then lunged upwards! The Flea gave a surprised squeak, and struggled in her arms.

'Got you!' cried Twink triumphantly. 'Mariella, look! I got him!'

Mariella's smile looked a bit strained. 'Glimmery.'

Still holding the struggling Flea, Twink skimmed across the field to Mariella. 'I think I'm ready to try out for Madge!' she cried excitedly. 'Don't you? The Forestglow game is tomorrow – Madge will be so relieved to have me back on the team!'

Mariella took the Flea from Twink and put him back in his cage. 'Yes, I – I suppose.'

Twink stared at her. 'What do you mean?'

Mariella smiled. 'Nothing. Forget I said anything. I think that's enough practice for today, don't you?' Grabbing up the cage, she skimmed quickly off towards where Lola waited for her on the sidelines.

'But –' Twink frowned in confusion, and then flitted after her.

Mariella and Lola were in a huddle on the sidelines, whispering together. As Twink drew closer, their voices carried across the grass.

'You mean you haven't *told* her?' demanded Lola.

'Shh! No, I haven't!' hissed Mariella back.

Lola shook her head. 'Well, I really think you ought to –'

'Tell me what?' asked Twink as she flew up beside them. Bewildered, she looked from one to the other.

Mariella scowled. 'Nothing! Lola, flap off!'

The thin little fairy gave a haughty sniff. 'Fine! But you know I'm right.' She flitted away, her pale blue wings wavering in the sunlight.

Twink's hands felt clammy. 'Um . . . what is she right about?'

'Nothing, I said!' Mariella's eyebrows drew together. 'Oh, Twink, just forget about it, can't you? I don't want to hurt your feelings!'

Twink stared at her. 'Hurt my feelings? How?'

Mariella flushed. 'Well, there's something I know, but – but I don't want to have to tell you.' Her eyes filled with tears. 'But now that Lola's let the moth out of the bag, I suppose I *have* to tell you, don't I?'

'Tell me what?' Twink shook Mariella's arm as they hovered. 'Mariella! What is it?'

'All right.' Mariella sniffed, wiping her eyes with the back of her hand. 'I – I didn't *want* to tell you this, but – well – I don't think you should go back to Madge about being on the team.'

Though it was a warm spring day, Twink suddenly felt like an icicle had dropped between her wings. 'Why not?'

'Because – because the rest of the team don't want you back!' blurted Mariella. 'Oh, Twink, I didn't want to tell you! But I *heard* them! They were saying the most awful things about how you play –'

'But I've got so much better now,' whispered Twink.

Mariella shook her head. 'They don't care. They don't trust you any more after the Sparklelight match. They want you off the team.'

'Oh.' Twink's wings slowed to a stop. She drifted downwards, landing on the ground. Her throat felt too tight to speak.

Mariella swooped down beside her. 'Oh, Twink, it's really mean of them!' she cried. 'After you've worked so hard, too. It's just not fair!'

'No – well – never mind,' muttered Twink. Suddenly she couldn't bear talking for a moment longer; she had to get away! 'I'll – I'll see you later!' she burst out, and took off into the air as fast as she could.

A smile spread across Mariella's face as she watched Twink fly away. Picking up the cage she peered at the Flea, waggling her finger through the bars at him. 'That didn't go badly at all, did it?' she said cheerfully.

'I don't believe it!' said Bimi, her blue eyes flashing. It was later that same day, and the two girls had just flown into the Great Branch for dinner. Drawing Twink to one side, Bimi propped her hands on her hips.

'Twink, you've gone completely mad if you trust Mariella for one single second! Have you actually *forgotten* what she's like?'

Bimi had seen how upset Twink was when she returned to school, and it hadn't taken much for her to get the whole story out of her friend. Now Twink

91

shook her pink head miserably as the rest of the school streamed past them, landing with skips and jumps.

'It's not like that, Bimi. I told you! She's – she's been really helpful, trying to get me back on the team again. Besides, the others haven't spoken to me since the Sparklelight match! It must be true.'

'Rubbish,' said Bimi. 'Why don't you just *ask* them?'

Twink felt the blood leave her face. 'Ask them?'

'Of course!' cried Bimi, flapping her wings. 'Honestly, Twink, you're ready to give up because of what *Mariella* said – so why not just ask the others if it's true? At least then you'll know!'

Twink looked doubtfully towards the upper-year tables. Mia and a few of the others on the team all sat together, at the Gardenia Branch table. Could she really get up the courage to go and ask them what they thought of her? She shivered.

Then Twink thought of her parents, and how proud they'd been when she made the team. She couldn't just give up without a fight, could she? She

straightened her wings.

'You're right!' she said. 'I'll do it, Bimi.'

'Good!' Bimi's face relaxed with relief. 'Go and do it now, Twink, before you lose your nerve.'

Twink started off across the Great Branch – and then turned back and hugged Bimi tightly. 'Thanks,' she whispered. 'And Bimi, I'm sorry that I've been such a wasp brain. You were right – about staying up too late, and about Mariella, and – oh, about everything!'

'Apologise later,' laughed Bimi. 'Go on, now – ask them!' She turned Twink around and gave her a push between the wings, propelling her towards the Gardenia Branch table.

Twink flitted off, weaving her way through the Great Branch. Her spirits rose as she watched Mia talking and laughing with the others. Oh, of *course* Bimi was right! Why hadn't she told her about all of this sooner? Mariella was obviously up to something, as usual. She'd been an idiot not to see it for herself!

Then Twink drew near enough to hear what Mia

was saying – and her heart plummeted straight into her pixie boots.

'I don't know why Madge ever let her on the team in the first place,' declared Mia, tossing her blue hair.

Pip nodded. 'I know. She's pretty awful, isn't she?'

'That's an understatement! She seemed like a good enough player at first, but ever since the Sparklelight match, it's been so obvious that she hasn't got what it takes –'

Twink couldn't bear to hear any more. Wheeling sharply away, she flew blindly back to her own table. The school butterflies were just streaming into the Great Branch as she slumped down on to her mushroom, fighting to hold back tears.

Sooze was holding a ribbiting contest with Sili and Zena, the three of them croaking for all they were worth. Pix was laughing, trying without success to referee.

'You lot are useless!' cried Sooze. 'Listen, this is how it goes.' She threw back her head. '*Ribbit! Ribbit croak ribbit!*'

'No!' shrieked Sili, choking with laughter. 'You've got it wrong – it's *ribbity croak croak*!'

'Seven out of ten to Sili,' said Pix. 'Zena, your turn!'

Under the cover of their laughter, Twink stole a look at Mariella, chatting to Lola at the end of the table. Mariella hadn't been up to anything after all. Every word she had said was true.

Twink's eyes pricked hotly as she told Bimi what had happened. Her friend rubbed her wing against Twink's, clearly lost for words. 'Maybe they didn't mean it quite so badly as it sounded,' she said weakly. 'Or –'

'They meant it all right,' said Twink. 'I'm – I'm not going to try out for the team again, Bimi. Mariella's right. Nobody wants me on it!'

'No, don't do that!' Bimi looked at Mariella, a slight frown creasing her blue eyebrows. Following her gaze, Twink saw that Lola's wings were shaking.

'But *Mariella*,' Lola whined. 'You said it was just –'

'Oh, hush! Stop going on about it.' Mariella shot

a glance at the rest of the table, and coloured up when she saw Bimi watching her. She bent her head close to Lola's again, whispering.

'Bimi? What is it?' asked Twink.

'I don't know,' said Bimi slowly. 'I just have a funny feeling about it, Twink. Don't decide just yet, anyway. Wait until after the match tomorrow, at least.'

Twink sighed as she picked at her seed cake. 'All right,' she said finally. 'I'll wait until after the match. But I don't see how it's going to make any difference!'

Almost the entire school turned out for the match the next day, crowding excitedly into the mushroom grandstand. Everyone wore their oak-leaf caps – even the older years, who usually left them off at every opportunity – and many carried bright oak-leaf banners with *GO GLITTERWINGS!* written on them with sparkling fairy dust. Even Miss Shimmery had one, and was waving it merrily.

Twink sat with the rest of Peony Branch,

watching as the teams warmed up on the field. The Forestglow side flitted about the poles like ghostly moths, looking wild and woodsy in their uniforms of papery white birch bark.

Twink spotted Mariella's silvery-green hair as she zoomed past, and a pang of envy stabbed her. Oh, she'd give anything if none of this had happened, and she was zipping about the field herself!

'Poor Twink. It should be you out there, not

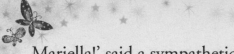

Mariella!' said a sympathetic voice.

Twink glanced up in surprise. Sooze was sitting on the mushroom just in front of her, and had twisted about on her seat, watching Twink's expression.

'It's my own fault I'm not,' said Twink shortly. She pretended to be fascinated by what was happening on the field. 'And anyway, I thought it was so *funny* that I fell asleep!'

'Oh, Opposite, don't be like that,' said Sooze earnestly, touching Twink's knee. 'I shouldn't have laughed. I'm sorry, all right?'

Twink's anger melted away like snow in the sunshine. She had missed Sooze – there was no one else quite like the lavender-haired fairy! 'All right,' she said with a smile. 'I – I suppose maybe I over-reacted a bit.'

Sooze laughed, fluttering her pink wings. 'No, you didn't! It was really awful of me. I promise I won't laugh again, Twink – even if I *don't* under-stand how you can care so much about a game!'

Twink sighed. Before she could tell Sooze that she

probably wouldn't be playing any more, Madge's reed whistle blew, and the match began.

Right from the start, the match seemed doomed. With the Forestglow team guarding him, the Flea sat preening himself in the sun, showing no signs of moving. Twink watched worriedly, clenching her fists. The Flea *would* choose today to behave himself! All the Forestglow Guards had to do was keep close to him, and tag anyone who came near. And it soon became clear that for every glimmery set piece the Glitterwings team had practised, Forestglow knew one in return.

Suddenly, in a quick, daring move, Mia darted from behind the pole and stole the Flea. 'HURRAH!' roared the crowd, leaping up and beating their wings together.

But Glitterwings still had to steal him twice more to win, and the Forestglow side were all excellent players. As the match turned in their favour they went on the attack, jetting about the field in blurs of white. One Glitterwings player after another was tagged, until finally only Mariella and Pip were left.

The Glitterwings crowd grew glum, their oak-leaf banners drooping.

'What happens *now*?' whispered Bimi in Twink's ear. The blue-haired fairy wasn't a Fledge fan, but even she looked tense and excited.

Twink shook her head. 'We're outnumbered – our only hope is to distract them, somehow, so that we can steal the Flea twice more!'

The words had hardly left her mouth when Pip, flying too fast around a post, collided hard with one of the Guards. She spiralled down to the ground, holding her head.

The crowd jumped to its feet again, murmuring in concern. Twink craned to see as Madge flew to Pip's side. A moment later, the Games Fairy led Pip off the field.

Oh, no! Twink sank numbly back down to her seat. 'We're a player short now!' she said to Bimi. 'That means we'll have to forfeit the game.'

Sooze spun about, her violet eyes flashing. 'Don't be daft, Twink! *You* could play!'

Twink gaped at her. 'But – but Madge said I'd

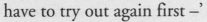

have to try out again first –'

'Well, I think she might change her mind *now*!' snapped Sooze. 'Go on, Twink. Get down there!'

Icy panic jolted through Twink. 'Sooze, I can't! The others have never forgiven me for the Sparklelight match. They all want me off the team!'

Out of the corner of her eye, Twink saw Lola's thin cheeks flush bright red from her mushroom seat a few places down. Lola glanced across at Twink, started to say something – and then stopped and looked quickly away.

Twink stared. What was up with her? But before she could lean across to ask, Bimi said, 'She's right, Twink. You've got to try, at least! We'll lose the match otherwise.'

Pix and the others chorused agreement. Bimi clutched Twink's arm. 'This is your chance to make it up to them! Don't you see? You have to play!'

Twink's wings felt weak. How could she play when the whole team hated her? But . . . but maybe the others were right. She gazed around her at the packed grandstands, and the worried faces of the school. Would she be letting everyone down if she didn't play?

She took a deep breath. 'All right,' she said. 'I'll talk to Madge.'

Chapter
Eight

Twink flew hurriedly down to the playing field. In the Games Fairy's box, Madge was leaning over Pip, giving the dazed fairy a drink of water from an acorn cup. Her broad face beamed with relief when she saw Twink.

'There you are!' she cried. 'Pip's going to have to go to the infirmary; she's got a nasty bump on her head. Can you play?'

Twink nodded reluctantly. 'I just need to get into my uniform. But – but Madge, there's something you should know. The rest of the team –'

'No time – tell me later!' said Madge, helping Pip to her feet. 'We've got a five-minute break – and then you're in!'

Twink kitted up as hastily as she could, and then skimmed out on to the Fledge field. The crowd cheered to see another player appear – but the cheers turned to buzzing whispers when the school saw who it was.

'Be sure you stay awake, Twink!' shouted a voice from the older years. Laughter rippled through the grandstand.

Twink's cheeks blazed. She couldn't bring herself to look at the rest of the team, sitting on the side-lines, though she could feel them all watching her. *Try not to think about them,* she thought fervently. *Just play the best you can!*

Mariella darted around a post and flew up to her. Her wings were sagging tiredly, and her silvery-green hair hung limply from its ponytail. Even so, she didn't look pleased to see Twink.

'Madge said she doesn't want you playing any

more than you have to,' she announced with narrowed eyes. 'So just keep the Guards away from me, and let *me* go for the Flea.'

Twink frowned uncertainly. 'But . . . she didn't tell *me* that. And I'm the faster flier –'

'Just do it!' ordered Mariella as the whistle pierced through the air. 'Or you'll be in even more trouble with the team than you already are!' She flew away, not waiting for an answer.

Almost immediately, one of the Forestglow Guards swooped towards Twink. Twink twisted away with a quick midair somersault, and felt a breeze brush past her foot where the Guard had almost tagged her. Phew! That was close.

The Flea still sat on the centre post, looking bored. A single Guard hovered beside it, while the remaining two zoomed about the field, intent on taking out Twink and Mariella. Twink ducked and dodged, avoiding them nimbly. Jetting around a post, she grinned as she heard one of the Guards give a frustrated squawk.

Glancing across at Mariella, Twink saw that the

pointy-faced fairy was trying to sneak up on the Flea from behind the centre post. *Come on, Mariella!* thought Twink. *You can do it!*

But the Guard spotted Mariella, swooping after her like an outraged moth. Mariella darted out of her reach. The other two Guards changed direction and also raced towards her, leaving Twink on her own at the end of the field.

Suddenly she gasped. The Flea was on the move! Apparently bored with sitting sunning itself, it bounded gleefully from post to post. The Guards gave an outraged howl. 'Quick, get it!' they shouted at each other.

The little grey insect leapt again, soaring high overhead. Twink shot up into the air, arrowing straight towards it. Her wings beat furiously, faster than she had ever thought possible. Only a bit more – almost there – now!

Just as the Flea started its descent, Twink lunged sideways at it, snatching it up in her arms.

'HURRAH!' screamed the crowd, leaping up and beating their wings. 'HURRAH FOR TWINK!'

She'd done it! Smiling broadly, Twink held the Flea over her head for a moment before skimming back to return it to the centre post. On the sidelines, Madge and the rest of the team were jumping up and down, hugging each other. Twink's heart soared.

'Nice move,' grinned one of the Forestglow girls as they all took their places again. 'But you won't get him again so easily, now that we know what he's like!'

'I told you to let *me* catch the Flea!' whispered Mariella as they waited for the whistle. Her green eyes flashed like angry emeralds.

Twink gaped at her. 'But he was right overhead! What was I supposed to do?'

Mariella turned away with a scowl as the whistle blew, and then the game was on again.

The Flea obviously had no intention of sitting still any more. It bounced wildly from post to post, and did little capers whenever it landed. Its Guards flew grimly after it, swooping and gliding.

Twink hovered closely behind a post, keeping out

of sight of the Forestglow team. If she got a chance to grab the Flea again, she'd take it, regardless of what Mariella said! The important thing was winning the game, not which one of them did it.

'And I bet Madge never said that anyway,' Twink muttered. She certainly hadn't looked angry after Twink had scored!

All at once Twink straightened. The Flea was heading right towards her, having lost its Guards with a frenzied series of leaps. All she had to do was jet upwards and grab him!

Twink darted out from behind her post. The Flea spotted her and abruptly changed direction, bouncing off the side of the post without landing. But Twink was too close to be shaken off easily, and she zoomed after him, hot on his tail.

The Guards swooped around a post, all three of them flying in unison as they barrelled towards her. *Don't think about them!* Twink put on a final burst of speed. The Flea was only a wing span away. Her fingers strained after him.

Suddenly she saw Mariella, racing towards the

Flea from the other direction. She had a look of almost agonised determination on her face, and Twink felt herself falter. *She must want to win really, really badly,* she thought.

Not entirely sure why she was doing it, Twink dived sideways at the last moment. Instead of tackling the Flea, she blocked his path so that he veered off towards Mariella. The other fairy reacted quickly, just as if they had planned it for years.

Swooping in like a hummingbird, Mariella grabbed the Flea from the air.

With a solid clap of sound the crowd went wild, screaming and cheering and waving their banners. Beaming triumphantly, Mariella held up the struggling Flea, basking in the applause.

'You did it,' said Twink, hovering beside her. 'Well done!'

An odd expression crossed Mariella's face. Her cheeks reddened as she looked at Twink. She started to say something, but before she could, the Glitterwings team burst on to the Fledge field, shouting excitedly.

'Hurrah!' cried Mia, throwing her arms around their shoulders. 'Oh, you two are the best reserves in the world! I was *sure* we were going to lose!'

'So was I!' bellowed Madge. She flew up grinning from ear to ear. 'Well done, both of you! And Twink, as far as I'm concerned, that was your try-out – and you passed it with flying colours. I want you back on the team!'

A warm glow spread through Twink. 'Oh, thank

you!' she cried. Then she remembered what she had overheard Mia say the night before, and her stomach tightened. 'But – but is everyone sure they really want me back?' she blurted out.

'Of course,' said Madge, looking puzzled. 'What are you talking about?'

Twink squirmed, wishing she hadn't said anything. 'It's just – well, I heard what you said to Pip last night,' she admitted to Mia. 'That you didn't know why Madge had ever let me on the team –' She stopped at the expression on Mia's face.

'Oh, Twink, we weren't talking about *you*!' cried Mia. 'Is that what you thought?'

'Who *were* you talking about, then?' Madge folded her arms across her chest.

Mia flushed under the Games Fairy's steady gaze. 'Well – we were talking about Mariella,' she admitted. She turned to the red-cheeked fairy.

'You're a good player, Mariella, but no one thought you had much team spirit, especially since the Sparklelight match – you seemed to care more about winning for yourself than playing with a team. But you've proved us wrong this match, you really have! That was a glimmery double move that you and Twink did at the end.'

Mariella nodded, looking a bit ill.

Twink struggled to take it all in. 'But – but no one spoke to me after the Sparklelight game! I thought –'

Mia shook her head in confusion. 'Mariella said that you were too embarrassed to face us, and we should just leave you alone until you got over it. We were watching you at the Sparklelight party, and you seemed so upset that we decided she was probably right.'

Twink stared at Mariella. The pointy-faced fairy gazed at the ground, not meeting her eyes.

She made it all up! thought Twink dazedly. All the snide things that she claimed the team had said – none of them had been true! The team had never hated her at all.

Mia looked from Mariella to Twink and back again. 'Twink . . . was she right?'

Twink swallowed. 'Um . . . sort of.'

'Well, you're playing like the old Twink again – that's the main thing!' Madge clapped Twink warmly on the shoulder. 'Now let's join Forestglow at the party. We deserve some fun after all the hard work we've put in!'

Twink glanced at Mariella. 'All right,' she said. 'I'll just . . . help Mariella put the Flea away.'

'Don't be too long. You two are the stars of the party!' Madge gave her a friendly wink and flew off towards Glitterwings. The team flitted along behind her, still chattering and laughing.

When everyone was gone, Twink looked at Mariella. The mushroom grandstand had almost emptied by now, and the Fledge field felt silent and expectant.

Flushing furiously, the other fairy avoided her gaze and swooped towards the ground. Still holding the Flea, Mariella grabbed up his cage from the side-lines, fumbling with the door.

Twink landed beside her, her heart beating hard. 'None of it was true, was it?' she said. 'All that stuff that you told me the team said, and that conversation I overheard between you and Lola . . .'

Mariella looked close to tears. Real tears this time, Twink realised, not the fake ones she had produced yesterday.

'So what if it wasn't?' she burst out.

'You'd better tell me the truth, Mariella,' said Twink in a low voice. 'Or I'll tell Madge and the others exactly what you said to me.'

Mariella paled. 'All right, it – it wasn't true,' she mumbled, looking away. 'I was just desperate to play more, that's all.'

Twink stared at her. 'What do you mean?'

'What do you think!' burst out Mariella. Shoving the Flea into his cage, she slammed his door shut and stood up. 'You're a better player than I am, that's what! I'd never get much of a chance with you around.'

It was the last thing in the world Twink had expected her to say. She slowly opened and closed her wings, at a complete loss for words.

Mariella swallowed, and continued. 'I thought Madge would throw you off the team if you messed up the Sparklelight match. That's why I tried to make you nervous about the set pieces, so you'd stay up all night studying and be too tired to play well.'

Twink's thoughts spun. 'You – you made me nervous on *purpose*?'

Mariella nodded, nudging the Flea's cage with her pixie boot. 'But Madge gave you a second chance, so I tried to get you to leave by telling you everyone was talking about you . . . only it didn't seem to work. Then when Madge took you off the team, I knew you'd just get Sooze or someone to help you practise, and then you'd be back again, taking all the moves away from me as usual! So I decided it was the perfect chance to gain your trust and make you leave for good.'

Twink stared at her, unable to speak. Mariella's cheeks burned bright red as she continued. 'So – so I offered to help you practise myself. And then I told Lola I was playing a joke on you, and that she had to pretend I was keeping a secret from you. She wasn't very pleased when she found out it wasn't a joke!'

Twink felt as if Mariella had punched her. 'But I – I thought that we had sort of got to be friends . . .' She trailed off.

'I suppose you're going to fly off and tell everyone now, aren't you?' Mariella demanded. Her eyes looked red and swollen. 'Then you can get *me* thrown off the team.'

'No, I wouldn't do that,' said Twink quietly. 'Mariella, you're a good player, too, you know. And – and don't you know what an awful trick that was to play? It was terrible, thinking that everyone hated me!' She clenched her fists, remembering.

Mariella winced, and nodded. 'I know. I – I'm sorry. I really am, Twink.'

And all at once Twink believed her. Mariella, who had been a trial to live with since the first moment Twink had met her, was actually apologising. Twink let out a breath she hadn't known she was holding.

'All right,' she said softly. 'I forgive you.'

The two fairies stared at each other. In the silence of the empty Fledge field, a bumblebee bobbed past, humming to itself. Finally Mariella made a face. 'Well . . . what happens now?'

Twink lifted a shoulder. 'We'll both stay on the team, I suppose. And maybe we'll never be friends off the Fledge field, Mariella, but can't we at least try to get along on it? I think we play together pretty well, when we try!'

Mariella nodded slowly. 'Yes, OK. Deal.'

On impulse, Twink held out her hand. Mariella

hesitated, and then shook it firmly. Suddenly she smiled. 'Come on, let's go to the party – I'm dying for some fizzy dew!'

That night in the second-year Common Branch, Bimi and Twink sat on the window seat together, looking out at the star-filled sky. 'I *knew* she was up to something!' said Bimi, shaking her blue head. 'Well, you're a lot nicer than I am, Twink. I'm not sure I could have forgiven her for such a mean trick!'

Twink glanced across the branch at Mariella. She stood flushed and radiant at the centre of a group of admirers, describing the final move of the game once more. And for once, she wasn't putting on airs or acting stuck-up – she just seemed happy.

Even so, Twink smiled to herself as she saw Sooze sitting crouched at a mushroom desk with her hands over her ears! Not everyone wanted to hear about Mariella's triumph, that was clear. But some fairies did . . . and that seemed to be enough.

'I feel sorry for Mariella,' Twink admitted, playing

with the edge of her peony dress. 'She just wants to be admired, but she always goes about it in the wrong way. She's really not so bad, Bimi. Or at least, I don't think she is deep down.'

Bimi gave her a sideways look. 'Is that why you let her catch the Flea?'

Twink's wings clapped together in surprise. 'How did you –'

Bimi laughed. 'I know the way you fly, Twink! You could have got the Flea easily. So why did you do it?'

Twink sighed and dropped her chin on her hand, gazing out at the large oak leaves rustling in the evening breeze. 'I don't know,' she said. 'She just . . . seemed to need it more than me.'

'You're daft,' said Bimi affectionately, tucking her arm through Twink's. 'Nice, but daft!'

'Thanks – I think.' Twink grinned at her best friend. It had been such a wonderful day! She was back on the team again, she had scored a point in front of the whole school . . . and she and Mariella had even reached a truce of sorts.

'Oh, look how tired that star looks,' said Bimi suddenly, pointing at the night sky. 'We can practise making a shooting star!' She laughed at Twink's puzzled expression. 'You weren't paying attention in that lesson, were you? Too busy with your strategy book!'

She explained what Mrs Starbright had taught them. Twink sat up straight, excitement tickling her wings. 'OK! Let's try it.'

The two fairies focused hard on the feebly shining star. *It's all right for you to leave if you like*, thought Twink, furrowing her forehead in concentration. *You can turn to star dust and come back as a new star!*

'Ooh!' she gasped, clutching Bimi's arm.

The star had become a jubilant arc of light, tracing its way across the glittering sky. Down . . . down . . . and then gone, with a final, joyful sparkle that seemed to wave goodbye.

'That was so beautiful,' murmured Bimi.

Twink nodded wordlessly, and the two friends smiled at each other. Pulling her knees to her chest, Twink leaned against the bark wall and gazed about

121

the Common Branch. Contentment spread through her like warm honey.

Yes, today had been wonderful . . . but really, the most wonderful thing of all was being a second-year student at Glitterwings Academy – the most glimmery school in the world!

The End

From Term-Time Trouble

Drip! Drip!

Twink Flutterby groaned to herself as she flew along behind her parents. The rain had been drumming down all day, and showed no signs of stopping. What an awful start to the new term!

'Hold your umbrella higher!' called Twink's mother. 'Your wings are getting wet.'

'*Everything* is getting wet,' grumbled Twink, adjusting her rose-petal umbrella. Beads of silvery rain formed on its edge, racing off it like pearls. Twink shook it grumpily. 'I bet Glitterwings has floated away by now.'

Her father laughed. 'Oh, I think you'll find it's still there. Your school has seen worse rain than this in its time!'

Twink's spirits lifted as Glitterwings Academy came into view. The massive oak tree sat calmly on its hill, its rich green leaves shiny with rain.

Titania Woods

There are lots more stories about Glitterwings
Academy – make sure you haven't missed any of them!

☐	Flying High	978 1 4088 0486 5
☐	Midnight Feast	978 0 7475 9209 9
☐	Friends Forever	978 0 7475 9208 2
☐	Fairy Dust	978 0 7475 9207 5
☐	Fledge Star	978 0 7475 9206 8
☐	Term-Time Trouble	978 0 7475 9205 1
☐	New Girl	978 0 7475 9204 4
☐	Seedling Exams	978 0 7475 9203 7
☐	Christmas Fairy	978 0 7475 9835 0
☐	Sister Secrets	978 0 7475 9831 2
☐	Treasure Hunt	978 0 7475 9832 9
☐	Friendship Dance	978 0 7475 9833 6
☐	Magical Mayhem	978 0 7475 9834 3

Coming soon:

☐	Power Play	978 1 4088 0269 4
☐	Fairy in Danger	978 1 4088 0268 7

If you have any difficulty in finding these in your local bookshop,
please visit www.bloomsbury.com or call 020 7440 2475
to order direct from Bloomsbury Publishing.

Visit www.glitterwingsacademy.co.uk for more fabulous fairy fun!